Jo, Charlie, Mum and Dad followed Catherine as she went up to the kennel. As she saw the little dog inside, Jo gasped. Sitting behind the wire mesh, barking as hard as he could, was a tiny ball of yellow fluff! As Jo looked in, the little dog jumped to his feet. "Woof!" He barked in relief, as if he was saying, *There you are, I've been waiting for you!* Jo stared at his floppy ears and deep brown eyes. He was the most gorgeous dog she'd ever seen!

Have you read all these books in the
Battersea Dogs & Cats Home series?

BUDDY AND HOLLY'S
story

by
Sarah Hawkins

Illustrated by Sharon Rentta
Puzzle illustrations by Jason Chapman

RED FOX

BATTERSEA DOGS & CATS HOME: BUDDY AND HOLLY'S STORY
A RED FOX BOOK 978 1 849 41416 6

First published in Great Britain by Red Fox,
an imprint of Random House Children's Books
A Random House Group Company

This edition published 2011

1 3 5 7 9 10 8 6 4 2

The Random House Group Limited supports The Forest
Stewardship Council (FSC®), the leading international forest
certification organisation. Our books carrying the FSC label are
printed on FSC® certified paper. FSC is the only forest certification
scheme endorsed by the leading environmental organisations,
including Greenpeace. Our paper procurement policy can be
found at www.randomhouse.co.uk/environment

MIX
Paper from
responsible sources
FSC® C016897

Set in 13/20 Stone Informal

Red Fox Books are published by Random House Children's Books,
61–63 Uxbridge Road, London W5 5SA

www.**kids**at**randomhouse**.co.uk
www.**totallyrandombooks**.co.uk
www.**randomhouse**.co.uk

Addresses for companies within The Random House Group Limited
can be found at: www.randomhouse.co.uk/offices.htm

THE RANDOM HOUSE GROUP Limited Reg. No. 954009

A CIP catalogue record for this book is available from the British Library.

Printed and bound by CPI Group (UK) Ltd, Croydon, CR0 4YY

Turn to page 89 for lots
of information on
Battersea Dogs & Cats Home,
plus some cool activities!

❖ ❖ ❖ ❖

Meet the stars of the Battersea Dogs & Cats Home series to date . . .

Bailey

Misty

Chester

Rusty

Daisy

Max

Snowy

Stella

Angel

Huey

Cosmo

Alfie

Buddy and Holly

Coco

A Christmas Surprise

"Brrrrr, it's SO cold!" Jo Clarke cried, rubbing her arms as she waited for her mum to unlock the front door. The bells on the Christmas wreath jingled as the door swung open, and the heat from the house flooded out.

"Everyone inside quick!" Mum urged. Charlie, Jo's four-year-old brother, hung round Mum's legs, but Jo and her best friend, Helen, didn't need to be told twice. They rushed into the warm and pulled off their thick winter coats.

"Come and see my Advent calendar!" Jo grinned at Helen, leaving her coat in a heap on the floor. "It's got baby animals on it!"

"OK!" Helen smiled, hanging her coat neatly on the hook, then picking up Jo's as well.

"I'd better find some treats for you two little superstars," Mum called as they sprinted up the stairs. "How about some mince pies and a mug of hot chocolate?"

"Yes please!" Jo yelled down as they dashed into her room and flopped on her bed. "That was so much fun!" she laughed. "Did you see when Peter tripped over his costume? The three wise men fell down like dominos!

Helen giggled. "I didn't even notice – I was too busy trying to remember my words!"

Jo smiled. Helen had played Mary in the school Nativity, and Jo knew how nervous she'd been. "You were brilliant," she told her friend.

"So were you!" Helen reached over and hugged her. "Your solo was amazing!"

"Yes it was!" Mum
agreed as she came in,
holding a plate of
mince pies and two
huge mugs of hot
chocolate, each topped
with a heap of squirty cream
and lots of marshmallows. Jo looked
at her mug and licked her lips. "Yum!
Thanks, Mum!"

Helen took a slurp and sighed happily.
"Thanks, Mrs Clarke!"

As she sipped her creamy chocolate
drink, Jo showed Helen her Advent
calendar. Under every flap was a different
animal wearing a Christmas hat.
"Wouldn't one of those be the best
Christmas present ever?" Jo asked,
already knowing the answer. She and
Helen were different in lots of ways –

Helen was really tidy and Jo couldn't help being a mess. Helen always remembered everything she needed for school, which meant that she usually had a spare pen or pair of PE socks to lend Jo when she forgot! They even looked completely different – Helen had freckly, pale skin and red hair and Jo had black hair and skin the same colour as the hot chocolate she was drinking – but they both loved animals and longed for a pet of their own.

"Oh yes! A kitten!" Helen sighed. "A tiny baby kitten! A stripy one, with soft fur and long whiskers.

Cats are the best, you can stroke them
and they curl up and sit on your lap."

"No way, dogs are the best!" Jo
declared. "You can cuddle them too, *and*
you can take them for
walks!"

"But you have
to pick up their
poo!" Helen
screwed up her
face as if she'd
eaten something
horrible. Jo bashed her with a pillow and
Helen squealed with laughter, grabbing
another one to swing back at Jo.

"Cats are way better than slobbery old
dogs!" Helen said.

"My dog wouldn't be slobbery!" Jo
attacked her again and they both
collapsed on the bed in a fit of giggles.

"What's all this about then?" Mum poked her head round the door. Jo and Helen laughed.

"We were just trying to work out which are better, dogs or cats," Jo explained breathlessly.

"Well, that's a coincidence," Mum said with a mysterious smile. Jo looked at her curiously.

"You'll see!" Mum grinned. "Your mum's downstairs, Helen. She's finished her Christmas shopping and she's come to pick you up."

Jo looked at Helen in surprise. Since they lived next door to each other, their parents usually let them go back and forth between their houses without worrying about coming to walk them home.

Helen shrugged, and they both followed Jo's mum downstairs. "The best thing would be if *you* got a dog and *I* got a cat," Helen decided practically. "Then we could share them!"

They went into the kitchen where
Helen's mum was sitting with Christmas
shopping bags piled up round her feet.
Mum sat next to her and pulled Charlie
onto her lap. He
snuggled up to her,
sucking his thumb.

"There's my
girl!" Helen's
mum smiled,
opening her
arms up for
a hug. "You
were such a
wonderful
Mary! I cried!"

"Aw, Mum!" Helen blushed.

"Sit down a minute, girls." Jo's mum
leaned forward excitedly. "We want to
talk to you about something."

Jo sank into the chair next to her mum, who looked so excited, like she had a secret and she was going to burst if she didn't tell them!

Mum smiled at Jo and Charlie. "I was going to wait until your dad got home but I just can't! We've got a big surprise for you guys! We've decided that you're old enough now to get something you've wanted for a long time . . ."

Jo's heart was racing. She glanced at Helen, who crossed her fingers and smiled hopefully.

"We're getting a puppy!" Mum shrieked, clapping her hands together in delight. Jo gasped. Charlie's eyes grew wide and his thumb popped out of his mouth. "A real one?" he asked.

"Yes, a real live one!" Mum told him. "Won't that be nice?" Charlie nodded.

"That's SO great!" Helen said, hugging Jo.

Jo couldn't believe it. "You can still share him," she said immediately, not wanting her friend to feel left out.

"Well, you might not have to," Helen's mum smiled. "Because WE are going to get a kitten!"

"I can't believe you two were just talking about it!" Mum added.

"I'm getting a kitten?" Helen gasped in shock. Jo saw her eyes fill up with happy tears. "I can't believe it!"

"It's just what we wanted!" Jo squealed. "It's a Christmas miracle!" She grabbed Helen and they jumped up and down together, laughing in delight.

"Well, they're not really for Christmas," Mum told them seriously, "because they'll need lots of love and looking after all year round, but we thought how nice it would be to have them in time for the holidays. Then you can spend lots of time playing with them and helping them to settle in before you have to go back to school."

"I'll love my puppy every day of the year, Mum!" Jo smiled. Her grin grew even broader as she thought about all the fun she'd have with Helen and their new pets. They could take her puppy for walks, and play games with Helen's kitten. This Christmas was going to be better than she could have ever imagined. As Jo looked at Helen, Helen turned to her with an enormous smile, her brown eyes wide. It looked like her best friend was thinking exactly the same thing!

Perfect Pets

"Everybody up!" Dad shouted from the hallway. "It's an important day today!"

Jo stretched in bed. *But the play was yesterday*, she thought. She'd been having the nicest dream, all about getting a puppy of her very own. Suddenly she remembered – it wasn't a dream! Today she, Mum, Dad, Charlie, and Helen and her mum were all off to find their pets!

Last night Mum and Dad had explained that they were going to go to Battersea Dogs & Cats Home, where lots of cats and dogs were looked after until they found people to give them their forever homes.

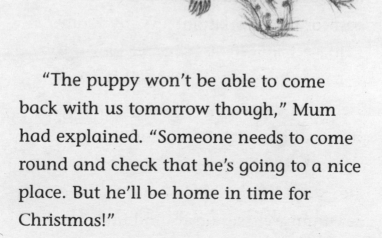

"The puppy won't be able to come back with us tomorrow though," Mum had explained. "Someone needs to come round and check that he's going to a nice place. But he'll be home in time for Christmas!"

Jo jumped up, scattering her pillows everywhere, and rushed over to her window. When they'd moved in and she had realized she could see across right into another girl's room she'd just known they'd be friends! Her room would never be as clean and tidy as Helen's was though. She flung open her curtains. Helen was sitting on her neatly-made bed, combing her hair. She was wearing her favourite green dress – she obviously wanted to look her best for her new kitten!

Helen spotted Jo
and waved her hairbrush,
then pointed downstairs. Jo
nodded, and grabbed the first clothes
she could see. She just couldn't wait to
go to Battersea and find her puppy!

"Come on everyone, get dressed!" Jo
yelled as she ran along the hallway into
Mum and Dad's room. "Helen's already
ready!"

Charlie was sitting next to Mum in
bed, watching cartoons in
his pyjamas. Jo leaped
on to the bed next to
him. "Hurry up!
We're going to get
our puppy!"

"Can't I go like
this?" Charlie asked,
looking down at his robot pyjamas.

"No you can't!" Mum laughed and
tickled his tummy. "But don't rush, we've
got plenty of time. And
you've got time to go
up and get
changed, Missy,"
she said to Jo.
"You've got odd
socks on and your
T-shirt's on inside-out!"

It was half-past ten before Mum finally
let Jo call round at Helen's house. Helen's
mum opened the door and smiled when
she saw her daughter's friend hopping
about impatiently. "Well, someone's
excited!" she grinned. "Come on inside,
it's too cold to be standing on the
doorstep."

"Areyoureadytogonow?"
Jo said in a rush.

"I'm ready!" Helen
called from the
hallway, peeking out
from behind her
mum. "Can Jo come
in the car with us,
Mum?" she pleaded.
"We need to talk about
what kind of cat and
dog we're going to get.

It's very important to be prepared," she added, seriously.

"Actually, *we're* going to go with Jo." Helen's mum smiled. "We're only going to *visit* our pets today, so Jo's mum's got enough room in the people-carrier for everyone. Are you ready now, Helly?"

"Yes!" Helen said impatiently, "let's go!"

Mum, Dad and Charlie were already waiting in the car, with the heating on full-blast. Jo and Helen slid into the two seats at the very back of the people-carrier, and Helen's mum, sitting next to Charlie, passed them a blanket to put over their knees.

"I really want a stripy kitten," Helen said dreamily.

"The stripy ones are called tabby cats," Helen's mum said.

"If you get an orange one it'll really look like part of the family!" Jo smiled.

"Oh yes!" Helen laughed, twirling her red hair round her finger. "What kind of dog do you want?"

"I don't know!" Jo sighed. "I was trying to think last night, but then I fell asleep."

Helen laughed. "I'm sure you'll know your puppy when you see it," she said reassuringly.

Just then, *Rudolph the Red-Nosed Reindeer* began playing on the radio and Charlie started singing along, loudly. Jo and Helen laughed, then joined in. Soon everyone in the car was singing at the tops of their voices.

Eventually the sat nav gave a bleep and announced, *You have reached your destination*. Mum parked the car and Jo jumped out into the frosty afternoon. It was so cold that her breath made clouds in the air. "Battersea Dogs & Cats Home is just over there," Mum pointed out. "See the sign?"

Charlie leaped out of the car and tore around excitedly. "I saw twenty-seven plastic Santas on the way here!" he shouted. "And fourteen Rudolphs!" he added, starting to sing again. Once Mum had calmed him down enough to put his scarf and gloves on, both families set off for Battersea Dogs & Cats Home.

As they walked up, Jo and Helen squeezed each other's hands. "I'm nervous!" Jo whispered.

"Me too," Helen admitted. "But I'm really excited as well!"

"Right, the cattery is this way," Helen's mum pointed at a tall, curved building near the entrance.

"And I think the reception is through here," Mum told Jo and Charlie.

"See you in the reception later?" Helen asked.

Jo nodded. "When we meet up again," she called excitedly, "we'll have met our perfect pets!"

Finding Buddy

Jo waved goodbye to Helen and her mum and walked into the reception. Mum grabbed her hand and gave it a little squeeze. "It's time to go and choose our puppy!" she whispered excitedly to Jo and Charlie.

"Can we call him Rudolph?" Charlie asked.

"Maybe,"Dad smiled. "Let's wait and

see if he already has a name. You
wouldn't like it if we changed your name
to Rudolph, would you?"

"I *would*," Charlie grumbled as they
walked up to the desk.

They were met by a tall lady called
Catherine. She had dog fur all over her
jumper, like she'd been hugging a wriggly
puppy. *Since she works at Battersea Dogs &
Cats home, she probably has been!* Jo
thought with a grin.

Catherine asked them about what kind of dog they were looking for and how big their house was, then she led them through the echoey corridors to a room with kennels on both sides. Charlie raced ahead with Dad, but for once Jo walked slowly, holding Mum's hand. She looked in each cage carefully. After all, the next dog she saw might be *her* puppy!

Suddenly a dog in one of the kennels at the end of the hallway started barking again and again. "Oops, I'd better go and check on Buddy," Catherine smiled, "he doesn't normally bark like that."

Jo, Charlie, Mum and Dad followed Catherine as she went up to the kennel. As she saw the little dog inside, Jo gasped. Sitting behind the wire mesh, barking as hard as he could, was a tiny ball of yellow fluff! As Jo looked in, the little dog jumped to his feet. "Woof!" He

barked in relief, as if he was saying, *There you are, I've been waiting for you!* Jo stared at his floppy ears and deep-brown eyes. He was the most gorgeous dog she'd ever seen!

"Mum, Mum," Charlie tugged on his mum's sleeve. "He looks just like the puppy on the toilet-roll adverts!"

Catherine laughed. "Well yes, the Andrex puppy is a golden Labrador and so is Buddy! We called him that because he's everyone's friend. Do you want to stroke him?" She opened the cage and let them in. Buddy trotted over with his tail wagging, looking really happy to see them! Jo crouched down and Buddy gave her face a big lick.

"That's funny," Catherine smiled. "He's stopped barking now you're here. I think he was calling you."

Jo stroked Buddy's gorgeous floppy golden ears and he rolled over so that she and Charlie could tickle his tummy. "Hello, Buddy," she whispered as she stroked his soft fur. "Were you waiting for us to come and get you?"

"Woof!" Buddy barked happily.

"Aw!" Jo looked up at her mum and dad.

"We ought to go round and look at the other dogs, Jo, to make sure he's the one we want," Dad said sensibly. "There are lots of dogs here, after all."

But Buddy was special. Jo just knew it. He had been waiting for them. She started to follow her family out of the pen, but Buddy trotted after her, barking again and again, his chocolate-brown eyes pleading. Jo sat down and put her arms round the little pup.

"I don't need to see any of the others," she said firmly. "I know Buddy's the one I want."

"Me too!" Charlie laughed as Buddy's tail wagged furiously.

"It does seem like he wants to be with us, doesn't it?" Mum smiled. Jo held her breath.

"I was only saying we should make sure." Dad shrugged. "But if you're certain . . ." He grinned at Catherine. "I think we've found our puppy!"

Jo laughed. "No Dad," she told him as she gave Buddy a gentle hug. "We didn't find him – he found us!"

An Early Christmas Present

Helen and her mum were already waiting at the reception when Jo and her family got there. "We'd better get a move on," Mum said, staring up at the grey sky. "It looks like it might snow."

As they drove home, Helen told Jo all about Holly. "The Battersea lady, Meg, took us to a room full of cat toys," she

described, her eyes shining.
"Then she went away
and came back with
three beautiful
kittens! Their
mum came
trotting in at
Meg's feet,
making sure her
babies were OK.
Then Meg put them
down and they all
started running around.
Holly – that's *my* cat," she added proudly,
"was playing with this toy and her sister
tried to take it, and Holly put out her
little paw and bopped her on the nose!"

Jo giggled.

"*And* she's a tabby cat." Helen
continued. "Because she's got a stripy coat."

"Show Jo the photo," Helen's mum reminded her.

"Oh yes!" Helen squealed. Jo had never seen her friend so excited! She showed Jo a photo she'd taken on her mum's phone.

"Oh she's *gorgeous*!" Jo shrieked. "I wish I'd taken a picture of Buddy."

"Well, I'll see him soon!" Helen grinned.

"I just can't believe they're called Buddy and Holly!" Dad laughed.

Jo and Helen looked at Charlie, who shrugged. Their parents smiled. "Buddy Holly was the name of a singer," Mum explained. "It looks like these two are destined to be friends!"

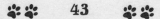

"I wish Buddy was here now," Jo sighed, "I feel really bad leaving him behind."

"I wish I could take Holly home now too," Helen whispered. "But it'll give us lots of time to get everything ready for them. We need to get bowls and leads and toys. And it's their very first

Christmas, so we need to make it extra-special for them. Besides," she joked, "you might need to tidy your room before you let a puppy in it!"

"That's true," Jo giggled. "If I let Buddy in there now I might never find him again! We've got so much to do before they arrive!"

Jo sighed happily as she stared out of the window and started thinking about all the things she wanted to buy for Buddy. Christmas lights twinkled on every house they passed, making the night seem magical. *There must be Christmas magic in the air*, Jo thought happily. After all, something incredible had already happened – she was getting the puppy she'd always dreamed of!

*

The next few days were really busy. Someone from Battersea came to visit both their houses to make sure that they were safe for their new family members, and Helen and Jo's mums took them on a shopping trip to a pet store to choose collars, bowls and toys for their lucky pets. Jo felt like one of Santa's elves as she and Helen picked presents that Holly and Buddy would love. Jo even found a doggy stocking with a bone on it for Buddy to hang up for Santa. "What do dogs call Father Christmas?" she joked.

"What?" Helen asked with a grin.

"Santa Paws!" Jo burst out laughing. Both their mums groaned.

*

It was four days before Christmas when they were finally allowed to pick Buddy up. Helen and her mum had gone to get Holly the day before, and Jo was desperate to have Buddy home too! Dad went to get him while Mum, Jo and Charlie stayed at home to get everything ready for his arrival.

Jo shrieked as she heard the car pull up in the driveway. "He's here, Buddy's home!" she shouted excitedly. Charlie dropped his toys and rushed over to the window. Suddenly the door opened and the little puppy burst in, dragging Dad, who was holding his lead, behind him!

"Hello, Buddy!" Jo grinned, stroking his soft head and unclipping his lead.

"Woof!" barked Buddy, scampering over to Charlie, who dropped to his knees to pet him. Buddy climbed on his lap awkwardly, trying to lick his chin. Then he jumped off and started sniffing round the lounge, poking his nose under the Christmas tree to smell all the presents stacked underneath it.

"Phew!" Dad said as he hung up his coat. "It's really cold and icy out there."

"Look," Jo grinned, "Buddy knows he's a Christmas present!" Buddy was sitting under the tree in amongst all the other gifts, his tail making a thudding noise as it thumped against the brightly-wrapped boxes. He sniffed at the tree trunk.

"That's a Christmas tree," Jo told him.

"I decorated it!" Charlie said proudly.

"There's already a present for you in there somewhere, Buddy," Jo told him delightedly.

"Why don't you open it for him?" Mum smiled.

"Here, you do it, Charlie." Jo grinned at her little brother. He tore open the wrapping paper. Buddy  put his head on one side and his ears pricked up at the crinkling sound. Charlie pulled out a new blue collar, with a shiny silver tag hanging from it. "Look, Buddy!"  he showed the pup his collar and tag. "On one side it says *Buddy*, and that's our telephone number."

"That's in case he gets lost," Mum explained. "Don't worry," she reassured Charlie, "he won't, but it's just so that if he ever does, people will know to phone us. And what's on the other side?"

Charlie turned it over. "A paw print!" he exclaimed.

"Woof!" Buddy barked happily as Jo fastened the smart new collar round his neck. Then he jumped out from under the tree and padded off to explore the kitchen. Once she'd shown Buddy his bowl, lead and toys, and the tiny pup had gulped down a huge bowlful of food, Jo couldn't wait any longer. "Can I take him round to meet Helen and Holly now, *please* Mum?"

Mum smiled. "Let me just ring Helen's mum first and check that Holly's ready for visitors. And you can't stay long – Buddy needs to get used to being here. Things are still very new for him." She picked up the phone and dialled next door. Jo waited impatiently until Mum put the phone down and gave her a thumbs-up. "Holly's settled in nicely, so it's fine for you to go round. But make sure you keep an eye on Buddy – dogs and cats don't always get on that well!"

"I will!" Jo grinned, jumping up to kiss her mum on the cheek. "Come on, Buddy!" she smiled, patting her legs.

Buddy scrambled to his feet and trotted after her. He waited patiently while she clipped his new lead onto his collar, then ran excitedly to the door as she opened it. A bitingly cold wind blew in. "Brrrr, good thing we're only going next door!" Jo smiled down at the little yellow pup.

"Woof!" Buddy agreed.

It was only when she stood on Helen's doorstep and rang the bell that Jo started to feel nervous – what if Buddy and Holly really didn't like each other?

New Best Friends

Jo stood anxiously outside Helen's house. Buddy sniffed round the door eagerly and pulled on his lead. "Can you smell Holly?" Jo asked, bending down to stroke his soft ears. "She's Helen's new cat. I haven't even met her yet, but I've heard *all* about her. Helen loves her as much as I love you. You're not allowed to chase her, or bark at her, OK? She's a *friend*."

"Woof," agreed Buddy seriously. Then his ears pricked up and he put his front paws against the door. Seconds later, Helen opened it, her mum standing behind her, a little furry bundle in her arms and a big grin on her face.

"Aw!" Jo sighed as she caught sight of Holly. She was every bit as gorgeous as Helen had described, with tiny pointy ears and delicate brown stripes in her fur.

"Ooh!" Helen squealed as she looked at Buddy. "Hello, Buddy! Come in," Helen stepped back into the hallway. "Holly's not allowed outside just yet." She led Jo

and Buddy into the
lounge and Jo shut
the door behind
them. Buddy was
sniffing Helen's legs
curiously. He put his
paws on her knees
and gave a soft whine,

trying to get to the kitten in her arms.

"Remember Holly's a friend," Jo said
nervously, sitting down and pulling him
onto her lap. Helen bent down so that
Holly and Buddy could see each other.

The little kitten peeked
out over her arm. She
looked down at the
yellow dog, her ears
twitching and her
tail swaying slightly
from side to side.

Buddy strained in Jo's arms as she lowered him gently to the floor. Helen carefully put Holly down and sat down as well. Jo held her breath as their pets walked over to each other curiously. Buddy got closer and closer – and Holly put out a paw and bashed him on the nose!

Buddy jumped back in alarm. Jo laughed softly. "Oh, it's all right!" she reassured the little pup.

"Maybe I should have told *Holly* to be friendly!" Helen laughed.

"You're not going to be scared of
Buddy just because he's bigger than you,
are you?" Jo smiled at the
kitten. Holly stretched
out her tiny paws and
nudged her head
against Jo's hand.
"Oh, she's SO lovely!"
Jo sighed. Holly purred
softly as Jo stroked her,
but she was too interested in Buddy to sit
still and enjoy being petted. Buddy had
recovered and was watching Holly
curiously, his tail giving little wags.

They sniffed each other and then Holly
stalked away and made a neat jump onto
the sofa. She lay there, watching Buddy's
every move. Buddy turned to sniff at
Helen, who stroked his back. "He's not
slobbery at all," she said, smiling at Jo.

Buddy's tail wagged happily, and
Holly put her paw out again to try and
catch it. "Holly, don't tease Buddy!"
Helen laughed.

"Woof!" Buddy agreed.

Helen went to scoop Holly up off the
sofa, but before she could, the little cat
jumped – straight onto Buddy's back!
Buddy spun round in surprise, then raced
forward with Holly clinging on tightly.
"Buddy!" Jo shouted at the same time as
Helen called "Holly!"

Jo couldn't help laughing – Buddy
looked so confused! He turned in a circle,
Holly balancing on his back like a
cowboy.

"Woof!" Buddy barked, racing round
the lounge.

"What's going on?" Helen's mum
called from the other room. "Are you OK
in there?"

"Yes, Mum!"
Helen replied, as
Jo lunged to
catch the tiny
pup. She
grabbed him and
Helen plucked Holly
off his back. Helen's

mum appeared at the door and put her
hands on her hips as she saw them all on
the carpet, a pile of pets and people.

"Sorry, Mum," Helen giggled. "They're making friends!"

"So I see!" Helen's mum laughed. "But calm down a bit, we don't want to get them too overexcited. And be careful you don't knock into the Christmas tree, OK?"

Jo looked at Helen and giggled. Helen rolled over to stroke Buddy, who flopped down next to her with a doggy grin. Holly stalked over to him and sniffed his nose. "It looks like she's kissing him!" Jo giggled. Holly curled up next to Buddy and put one of her tiny paws on his.

"Awwww!" both girls cried.

"I'll go and get my camera!" Helen's mum said, rushing away.

Helen looked down at their pets and smiled. "I still think cats are best," she said as she ran her hand along Buddy's back and down his wagging tail, "but Buddy is the cutest dog I've ever met."

Jo grinned at her friend. "Well," she laughed. "I still think dogs are better than cats – but Holly is the cleverest cat ever. She's almost as good as a dog."

"Almost?" Helen scoffed, holding up a cushion as if she was going to throw it at Jo.

"OK, OK!" Jo smiled. "Holly's the best cat ever and Buddy is the best dog. And you," she added, trying to grab the cushion from Helen, "are the best friend!"

Partners in Crime

Once Helen's mum had taken lots of photos of them all in front of the Christmas tree, she called the girls into the kitchen for a snack. Jo sat happily at Helen's kitchen table, enjoying the yummy Christmassy smell of baking gingerbread men and watching their

pets scamper around playfully. Helen's mum gave them each a cup of hot chocolate. "It looks like you four are going to have lots of fun together," she said, ruffling Helen's hair.

"Do you want to take Buddy for a walk with us tomorrow?" Jo asked. "We're going to take him along by the canal."

"Yes please!" Helen grinned. "I wish Holly could come too! She's not allowed outside until she's had all her injections."

"When the weather's like this it's nice being inside, though," Helen's mum added, pulling some gingerbread men out of the oven and resting them on a wire rack on the table. "Tell you what, when you come back from your walk tomorrow I'll make a fire and you two can snuggle next to it with Holly and Buddy and watch a film."

"Brilliant!" the girls chorused.

"I know just what film Holly would like," Jo said. "*Aristocats!*"

They all laughed. Jo looked round for her little pup. He and Holly were being *very* quiet. Suddenly she saw a paw appear, stretching up to try and get one of the gingerbread men on the table. Jo gasped – how could Holly reach? She jumped up. "Helen *look!*" She giggled. Holly was balanced on Buddy's back!

Jo rushed towards them and the little
cat jumped as if she knew
she'd been caught doing
something naughty!
She nimbly leaped
down off Buddy's
back and started to
lick her paw
innocently, as if she
hadn't been doing
anything wrong.

"NO, Holly!"
Helen's mum scolded
her. "They're *hot*, you could burn your
paws, you silly cat."

"She *keeps* trying
to jump on the
work surfaces to
eat things," Helen
explained to Jo.

"She tried to eat a bit of my lunch earlier on. I can't believe she and Buddy were working together to try and steal a snack!"

"Uh-oh, maybe you should take Buddy home," Helen's mum suggested, chuckling. "Holly's obviously a bad influence on him."

"Naughty Buddy," Jo said, as the little puppy plodded over to her. He looked up at her with his big brown eyes and her heart melted. "Awww, I can't stay cross with him!" she giggled. "Isn't it good that they get on so well?"

"They're not just friends, they're partners in crime!" Helen joked.

Helen's mum smiled. "We'll have to keep a close eye on your naughty pets – who knows what they'll be up to next!"

Christmas Eve

Jo spent every second of the next few days with her beautiful new puppy. Dad, Jo and Helen, wrapped up like Eskimos, took Buddy for a walk in the park, then Jo and Buddy went round to Helen's to curl up on the sofa and play with Holly. Buddy trotted after Jo wherever she went, like her furry shadow. He even slept on the end of her bed at night!

By the time it was Christmas Eve, Jo
honestly couldn't imagine what her life
had been like without him. "Come on,
Buddy." She smiled down at him as he
sat at her feet. "We need to get Helen's
present wrapped
before she comes
round!" Jo got
to work cutting
and sticking,
while Buddy
helped by
chewing on
the roll of
Sellotape. They'd
just finished when the doorbell rang.

Jo and Buddy raced downstairs and
flung the front door open. Helen was
standing there, shivering in a big coat,
hat and a matching scarf. "Sorry I'm

late," she said, sounding flustered. "Holly just wouldn't let me leave! She kept winding round my legs and meowing for attention. I had to sneak away while she was in the other room with Mum, otherwise I never would have got here! Anyway, Merry Christmas!" she finished, holding out a beautifully-wrapped present with a huge pink bow on it.

"Ooh thanks!" Jo squealed. "Yours is upstairs, but I think I have to unwrap *you* first!" She helped Helen take off her coat and hung it on the hook.

"I got one for Buddy too – I don't think you'll be able to guess what it is!" Helen smiled, then pulled a bone-shaped present from behind her back.

"Woof! Woof!" Buddy barked excitedly, jumping up at Helen's coat.

"Your present's here, you big silly!" Helen joked, bending down to give it to him.

"He's more interested in your coat!" Jo laughed. "Come and get your present." The girls went up to Jo's room and she grabbed her present for Helen. It was a bit crumpled and covered with sticky tape, but Helen didn't look like she minded.

"Thank you!" she said, grinning.

"Oh, and I've got a
present for Holly as
well," Jo added,
holding out a
purple patchwork
toy mouse. "It's
got catnip in it."

"She'll love it!"
Helen smiled.

"I'll put my present
under the tree." Jo jumped up. "It's
funny," she told her best friend as they
started to go downstairs. "I am excited
about tomorrow, but I already feel like
Santa's come. I just can't imagine getting
any presents that will be better than
Buddy."

"I know just what you mean," Helen
grinned. "I love Holly *so* much. In fact, I

can almost hear her now!"

"I can hear something too!" Jo gasped.
"I think it's coming from downstairs." As
they raced downstairs the noise got
louder and louder. There was definitely
something happening in the front room.
Buddy was barking excitedly and there
were lots of tinkly noises, like tiny bells
. . . or the decorations on a Christmas
tree . . .

Jo ran into the lounge and gasped in
shock. There, clinging to the branches of
the Christmas tree by the tips of her
claws, was Holly! Buddy was leaping
around the base of the tree, barking
frantically. Holly scrambled up a few
more branches until she was right at the
top where the star should be.

"Holly!" Helen gasped. "What are you
doing here?"

"She must have come over with you somehow!" Jo gasped. "Your coat! Buddy was so interested in it – Holly must have been hiding inside!"

"What's going on?" Charlie yelled, skidding into the room. His noisy entrance startled Holly, and her paws slipped. Before Jo could move she was tumbling down the tree, bringing ornaments and tinsel with her as she scrabbled desperately to hold on to something.

"Holly!" Helen screamed as she lunged forward to try and catch her. But someone else got there first. As Holly dangled from a piece of tinsel, Buddy put his front paws up against the tree trunk and stretched up as far as he could go.

"Woof!" He barked at Holly, as his nose reached up to her struggling back paws.

The scared kitten
looked down at
him, then let go,
landing heavily
on his back.
Buddy gave a
muffled woof
as Holly
scrambled down
and raced straight
over to Helen for a
cuddle.

"Oh Holly!" Jo
cried out. "Buddy, you
saved her!" As Helen
checked Holly to make
sure she wasn't hurt, Jo
picked Buddy up for a cuddle.
"Is she OK?" Charlie said, worriedly.
"She's fine," Helen reassured him.

"Thanks to brilliant
Buddy!"

"Mum!" Charlie
raced out of the
room. "Guess what
just happened!
Buddy's a superdog!"

"Good boy, Buddy, good, good boy," Jo
whispered into his fur. His tail wagged so
fast it was a blur. "You brave puppy!" she
praised him. "You saved
Holly!" Buddy
sniffed at Holly,
who purred and
rubbed her face
against him.

"Holly's saying
thank you,
Buddy!" Helen
cried.

Mum came in wearing a snowflake jumper and a pair of reindeer antlers.

"Goodness me!" she gasped as Charlie told her what had happened, and she looked at the mess in the living room. "Thank goodness she wasn't hurt. I hope you've learned your lesson, Holly."

Holly peeked out from Helen's arms. "Miaow!" she replied. Mum laughed.

"Well, since you're a hero, I think you deserve to open one of your presents now, Buddy." Mum smiled. "And you too, Holly, since you've had a bit of an adventure. Come on, Charlie, it's time for you to be up in bed. Otherwise you-know-who won't come and deliver your presents!"

"OK!" Charlie rushed up the stairs.

"This is the only night of the year that he doesn't make a fuss about going to bed." Mum laughed as she followed him upstairs.

Jo rushed to give Holly her purple patchwork mouse, and Helen put Buddy's bone in front of him. Buddy didn't seem too interested until Jo tore off the wrapping paper for him and he could smell what was inside.

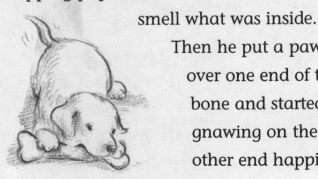

Then he put a paw over one end of the bone and started gnawing on the other end happily.

Holly sniffed at the mouse timidly. "It's
OK, Holly," Jo reassured her. She wiggled
the mouse from side-to-side and Holly
instinctively pounced on it.
Then she batted it
away and jumped
on it before
rolling on to
her back and
clawing it with
her feet,
making soft
purring noises.

Jo smiled down at their happy
pets, lying beneath the Christmas tree.
Then she gasped. "Look . . ." she cried.
"It's snowing!" The girls rushed to kneel
on the chair next to the window so they
could peer out into the dark night. In the
light from the lampposts they could see

fat white flakes fluttering down, coating their street with a layer of white.

"Merry Christmas," Jo whispered, putting her arm round Helen.

"Merry Christmas," Helen whispered back. There was a scrabble on the seat behind them, and Buddy squeezed in between them. Then Holly walked daintily along the back of the chair.

"And Merry Christmas to you too, Buddy and Holly!" Jo and Helen chorused.

Read on for lots more . . .

🐾 🐾 🐾 🐾

Battersea Dogs & Cats Home

Battersea Dogs & Cats Home is a charity that aims never to turn away a dog or cat in need of our help. We reunite lost dogs and cats with their owners; when we can't do this, we care for them until new homes can be found for them; and we educate the public about responsible pet ownership. Every year the Home takes in around 10,000 dogs and cats. In addition to the site in southwest London, the Home also has two other centres based at Old Windsor, Berkshire, and Brands Hatch, Kent.

The original site in Holloway

History

The Temporary Home for Lost and
Starving Dogs was originally opened in a
stable yard in Holloway in 1860 by Mary
Tealby after she found a starving puppy in
the street. There was no one to look after
him, so she took him home and nursed
him back to health. She was so worried
about the other dogs wandering the streets
that she opened the Temporary Home for
Lost and Starving Dogs. The Home was
established to help to look after them all
and find them new owners.

Sadly Mary Tealby died in 1865, aged
sixty-four, and little more is known about
her, but her good work was continued. In
1871 the Home moved to its present site
in Battersea, and was renamed the Dogs'
Home Battersea.

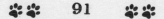

Some important dates for the Home:

1883 – Battersea start taking in cats.

1914 – 100 sledge dogs are housed at the Hackbridge site, in preparation for Ernest Shackleton's second Antarctic expedition.

1956 – Queen Elizabeth II becomes patron of the Home.

2004 – Red the Lurcher's night-time antics become world famous when he is caught on camera regularly escaping from his kennel and liberating his canine chums for midnight feasts.

2007 – The BBC broadcast *Animal Rescue Live* from the Home for three weeks from mid-July to early August.

Amy Watson

Amy Watson has been working at Battersea Dogs & Cats Home for six years and has been the Home's Education Officer for two and a half years. Amy's role means that she organizes all the school visits to the Home for children aged sixteen and under, and regularly visits schools around Battersea's three sites to teach children how to behave and stay safe around dogs and cats, and all about responsible dog and cat ownership. She also regularly features on the Battersea website – www.battersea.org.uk – giving tips and advice on how to train your dog or cat under the "Fun and Learning" section.

On most school visits Amy can take a dog with her, so she is normally accompanied by her beautiful ex-Battersea dog, Hattie. Hattie has been living with Amy for just over a year and really enjoys meeting new children and helping Amy with her work.

The process for re-homing a dog or a cat

When a lost dog or cat arrives, Battersea's Lost Dogs & Cats Line works hard to try to find the animal's owners. If, after seven days, they have not been able to reunite them, the search for a new home can begin.

The Home works hard to find caring, permanent new homes for all the lost and unwanted dogs and cats.

Dogs and cats have their own characters and so staff at the Home will spend time getting to know every dog and cat. This helps decide the type of home the dog or cat needs.

There are three stages of the re-homing process at Battersea Dogs & Cats Home. Battersea's re-homing team wants to find you the perfect pet: sometimes this can take a while, so please be patient while we search for your new friend!

1 Register details

2 Match

3 Leaving with your new pet

Have a look at our website: **http://www.battersea.org.uk/dogs/ rehoming/index.html** for more details!

"Did you know?" questions about dogs and cats

- Puppies do not open their eyes until they are about two weeks old.

- According to *Guinness World Records*, the smallest living dog is a long-haired Chihuahua called Danka Kordak from Slovakia, who is 13.8cm tall and 18.8cm long.

- Dalmatians, with all those cute black spots, are actually born white.

- The greyhound is the fastest dog on earth. It can reach speeds of up to 45 miles per hour.

- The first living creature sent into space was a female dog named Laika.

- Cats spend 15% of their day grooming themselves and a massive 70% of their day sleeping.

- Cats see six times better in the dark than we do.

- A cat's tail helps it to balance when it is on the move – especially when it is jumping.

- The cat, giraffe and camel are the only animals that walk by moving both their left feet, then both their right feet, when walking.

Dos and Don'ts of looking after dogs and cats

Dogs dos and don'ts

DO

- Be gentle and quiet around dogs at all times – treat them how you would like to be treated.
- Have respect for dogs.

DON'T

- Sneak up on a dog – you could scare them.
- Tease a dog – it's not fair.
- Stare at a dog – dogs can find this scary.
- Disturb a dog who is sleeping or eating.

- Assume a dog wants to play with you. Just like you, sometimes they may want to be left alone.
- Approach a dog who is without an owner as you won't know if the dog is friendly or not.

Cats dos and don'ts

DO
- Be gentle and quiet around cats at all times.
- Have respect for cats.
- Let a cat approach you in their own time.

DON'T
- Never stare at a cat as they can find this intimidating.

- Tease a cat – it's not fair.
- Disturb a sleeping or eating cat – they may not want attention or to play.
- Assume a cat will always want to play. Like you, sometimes they want to be left alone.

Some fun pet-themed puzzles!

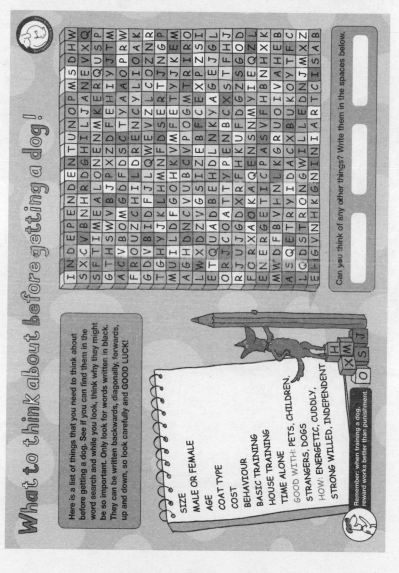

What to think about before getting a dog!

Here is a list of things that you need to think about before getting a dog. See if you can find them in the word search and while you look, think why they might be so important. Only look for words written in black. They can be written backwards, diagonally, forwards, up and down, so look carefully and GOOD LUCK!

SIZE
MALE OR FEMALE
AGE
COAT TYPE
COST
BEHAVIOUR
BASIC TRAINING
HOUSE TRAINING
TIME ALONE
GOOD WITH: PETS, CHILDREN, STRANGERS, DOGS
HOW: ENERGETIC, CUDDLY, STRONG WILLED, INDEPENDENT

Remember: when training a dog, reward works better than punishment.

Can you think of any other things? Write them in the spaces below.

Tangled Leads and Crazy Maze

Oh dear! The Battersea staff are walking three dogs but the leads are tangled. Can you find out which dog belongs to which person by following the leads?

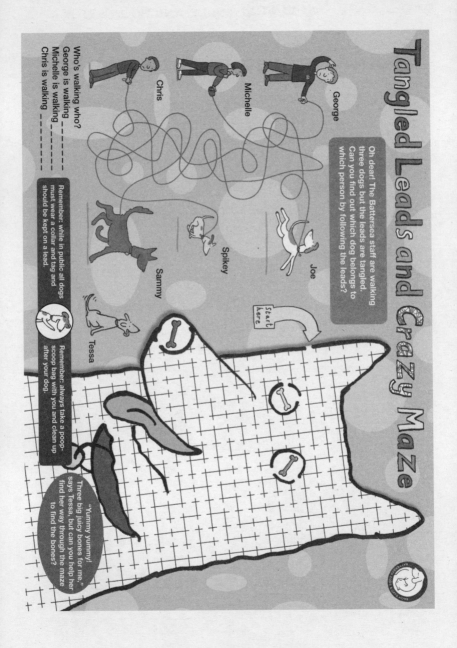

George

Michelle

Chris

Joe

Spikey

Sammy

Tessa

Start here

"Yummy yummy! Three big juicy bones for me," says Tessa, but can you help her find her way through the maze to find the bones?

Who's walking who?
George is walking _ _ _ _ _ _ _
Michelle is walking _ _ _ _ _ _
Chris is walking _ _ _ _ _ _ _

Remember: while in public all dogs must wear a collar and tag and should be kept on a lead.

Remember: always take a poop-scoop bag with you and clean up after your dog.

Drawing dogs and cats

If you can draw these shapes you can draw a dog:

head
ears
body
neck
front legs
back legs
tail

Draw your dog in pencil.

Use a pen to smooth the edges and add toes, collar and 'whisker dots.'

Rub out the pencil line.

Add shading/colour.

If you can draw these shapes you can draw a cat:

ears
face
body
front legs
back legs
tail

Draw your cat in pencil.

Use a pen to smooth the edges and add toes, collar and whiskers.

Rub out the pencil line.

Add shading/colour.

Dog Breeds Crossword

Across

2 A breed used as police dogs and sometimes called an Alsatian. (6,8)

5 A dog that is a mixture of breeds. (7)

6 A breed commonly used as guide dogs for the blind. (8)

9 Smallest breed of dog. (9)

11 A brown/liver and white breed often referred to as sniffer dogs. (8,7)

14 A French breed with very curly hair, traditionally used as a gun dog. (6)

15 A small black and tan terrier that was used to catch rats. (6)

16 A small white terrier from Scotland. (6)

17 A small breed with short legs and a long back, sometimes called a sausage dog. (9)

18 The dog often used as the symbol of Great Britain. (7)

Down

1 A spotted dog from a Disney film that needs lots of walking as a pet. (9)

3 A breed associated with a brand of paint. (3,7,8)

4 This breed is used to herd sheep and needs lots of activity such as agility if kept as a pet. (6,6)

7 Eddie from the programme *Frasier* is one of these. (11)

8 A breed associated with a brand of shoes. (6,5)

10 Scooby Doo was one of these very large dogs. (5)

12 These dogs are used for racing but also make good pets. (9)

13 Smaller version of "Lassie" dog. (7)

Help!

Ali is trying to count the dogs but some of them keep running about.
How many can you count?

Remember, all dogs need exercise in order to keep them fit and healthy and to give them mental stimulation.

Making a Mask

Copy these faces onto a piece of paper and
ask an adult to help you cut them out.

Fingerprint dogs and cats.

Thumb print over corner of scrap paper and remove to leave white triangle for nose and mouth.

Stick-on eyes: Hole-punched pieces of paper with dots marked in the centres.

Or use white paint to make eyes and tummy.

Cat Breeds Crossword

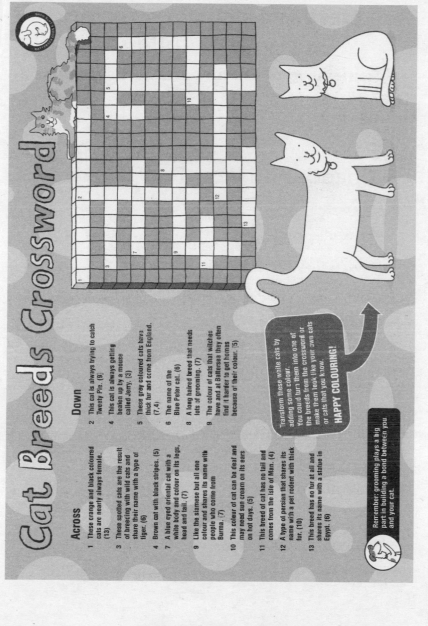

Across

1 These orange and black coloured cats are nearly always female. (13)

3 These spotted cats are the result of breeding with wild cats and share their name with a type of tiger. (6)

4 A blue eyed oriental cat with a white body and colour on its legs, head and tail. (7)

7 Brown cat with black stripes. (5)

9 Like the siamese but all one colour and shares its name with people who come from Burma. (7)

10 This colour of cat can be deaf and may need sun cream on its ears on hot days. (5)

11 This breed of cat has no tail and comes from the Isle of Man. (4)

12 A type of persian that shares its name with a pet rodent with thick fur. (10)

13 This breed has no fur at all and shares its name with a statue in Egypt. (6)

Down

2 This cat is always trying to catch Tweety Pie. (9)

4 This cat is always getting beaten up by a mouse called Jerry. (3)

5 These grey coloured cats have thick fur and come from England. (7,4)

6 The name of the Blue Peter cat. (6)

8 A long haired breed that needs lots of grooming. (7)

9 The colour of cats that witches have and at Battersea they often find it harder to get homes because of their colour. (5)

Transform these white cats by adding some colour.
You could turn them into one of the breeds from the crossword or make them look like your own cats or cats that you know.
HAPPY COLOURING!

Remember: grooming plays a big part in building a bond between you and your cat.

Here is a delicious recipe for you to follow.

Remember to ask an adult to help you.

Cheddar Cheese Dog Cookies

You will need:

227g grated Cheddar cheese
(use at room temperature)

114g margarine

1 egg

1 clove of garlic (crushed)

172g wholewheat flour

30g wheatgerm

1 teaspoon salt

30ml milk

Preheat the oven to 375°F/190°C/gas mark 5.

Cream the cheese and margarine together.

When smooth, add the egg and garlic and mix well. Add the flour, wheatgerm and salt. Mix well until a dough forms. Add the milk and mix again.

Chill the mixture in the fridge for one hour.

Roll the dough onto a floured surface until it is about 4cm thick. Use cookie cutters to cut out shapes.

Bake on an ungreased baking tray for 15–18 minutes.

Cool to room temperature and store in an airtight container in the fridge.

There are lots of fun things on the website, including an online quiz, e-cards, colouring sheets and recipes for making dog and cat treats.

www.battersea.org.uk